Other books by Raymond Bean

Sweet Farts #2: Rippin' It Old-School

Sweet Farts #3: Blown Away

Sweet Farts #1

Sweet Farts #1

RAYMOND BEAN

Visit www.raymondbean.com

amazon encore

Text copyright © 2010, Raymond Bean
All rights reserved.
Printed in the United States of America

Published by AmazonEncore
P.O. Box 400818
Las Vegas, NV 89140

ISBN-13: 9781612182506
ISBN-10: 161218250X

Interior illustrations by Ben Gibson
Author photo by D. Weaver

For Stacy, Ethan, and Chloe.
Also, for Baba, who would do anything for us.

Contents

Prologue

You know how it is at school...kids sneak "them" out in perfect silence so no one can tell who did *it,* or dealt *it,* or done *it*. *It* is a mystery, unsolvable, untraceable, sourceless. Then, as the awful stench begins to reach each nostril, kids begin to eye each other. Kids begin to take notice. Kids begin to wonder...

Who did it? they ask themselves silently. Of course, you can never be sure who did it, not in public. In public, everyone is a suspect. Everyone is potentially guilty.

When this most delicate of situations presents itself, the trick is not to look too surprised, even when you are *not* the one who laid it down. Overdoing your reaction can lead to unwanted suspicion. Your look has to be just right. It must show others that you are amused and offended at the same time. Shaking your head from side to side a little and closing your eyes in disbelief is a safe way to go. You cannot, however, under any circumstances, lose your cool. You must look confident. Remaining calm is essential.

I always try to smile, like I think it's funny, or make a face like I'm disgusted. These strategies come with some dangers though, because if you start to smile too much, you look guilty. And if you look too disgusted, guilty again.

We all know that the last thing you want to appear is guilty when there is a horrible, smelly fart loose in the room. In those first few moments after everyone gets a whiff, it's pure survival mode. Someone in the area is responsible, and everyone knows it. So, of course, it could be blamed on anyone. The person who did it isn't going to raise his or her hand and say, "It was me, everyone. I'm the one who just stunk up the place."

We all know that many innocent bystanders have been blamed for someone else's fart. And let's be honest: the kid who lets out a real stinker is usually the type of kid who is prepared to blame it on someone else. This is type of kid looks for that one person who gets embarrassed easily and then tries to cast suspicion his way. Once the "farter" casts suspicion on the embarrassed kid, no one stops to think it could be someone else. It happens every day, and it's tragic.

CHAPTER 1
The Cruelest of Fates

There is not much worse in this life than taking the blame for someone else's fart. It is an injustice as old as farts themselves, which must, I guess, be as old as human history. I'm sure people have been bouncing farts off the walls of dimly lit caves since the days of the caveman. Today, someone silently slipped one off a blue plastic chair in my fourth grade class, and I'm afraid it was my turn to take the blame. But it wasn't me...I swear.

I was at my desk for our morning class meeting. My teacher, Mr. Cherub, insists on meeting every morning to talk about our feelings and what is going on in our lives. He was just getting started when I realized something was wrong. I got a whiff of *it* before anyone else, but I couldn't be sure where *it* had come from. Panic immediately grabbed hold of me. My heart began to race. Something was wrong. Something was horribly wrong.

I took another sniff and my worst fears were confirmed. Someone dropped a stank bomb. And that somebody was the person right in front of me: Anthony Papas.

How could I possibly be expected to think or share my feelings with the stench of Anthony clobbering my nostrils? He turned around to check the clock on the wall behind us, and I gave him a look that conveyed, "You're killing me! Please don't do that *ever* again."

Anthony looked right at me and in front of everyone said, "You're gross!"

I couldn't believe it. People were actually staring at me with disgusted looks on their faces. Austin, who sits at the desk next to me, opened his eyes really, really wide and pointed at me. Tiffany, who sits in front of Austin, held her nose and put her face down on her desk. As I looked around the room, every kid in my class was gawking at me like I was responsible. Some smiled, some looked shocked, and some just shook their heads.

Now, I happen to be the kind of kid who embarrasses easily. The more eyes I felt on me, the more anxious I became.

"It wasn't..." I began.

Mr. Cherub interrupted me. "Is something wrong, Keith?" he asked.

Is something wrong? I thought. *Are you kidding me? This place is bombed to bits and everyone thinks it was me!*

Just then, Anthony raised his hand.

"Mr. C."

"Yes, Anthony?"

"I think Keith might be a little sick...you know, in the belly?" he said, while rubbing his hand in a circle on his stomach and making a face like he had a bellyache.

I could tell by the way Mr. C. was scrunching up his face that the smell had just reached him.

"Keith, umm...do you need to excuse yourself?" he asked as he held his hand to his nose and fought back a gag.

I didn't know what had happened! I couldn't move, I couldn't speak, I couldn't think. I just sat there and shook my head back and forth. You could have heard a pin drop. It was so quiet I could actually hear the sound of the heater by the window. I heard the ticking of the clock.

"Okay. Next time, just head on down to the bathroom," Mr. Cherub quickly added.

I don't know what it feels like to have a heart attack, but I'm pretty sure I was having one. My eyes must have been three times their size. They felt as if they might fly out of my head. And then Anthony said, "It's okay. It happens to the best of us, Keith."

"But it wasn't..." I began.

"That's enough," Mr. C. said. "Let's get back to work. Next time, please use the bathroom, Mr. Emerson."

We did get back to work, and everyone still thought it was me. I don't know why I didn't speak up. I could not believe that I was the one everyone thought did it. This was not good at all. I'm not the kind of guy who can pull something like that off. Some guys can laugh it off like it doesn't bother them. Not me; I don't have that kind of confidence. I'm not someone who can think real fast in moments like that either. My mind becomes paralyzed. I lock up. It was like my mouth had frozen shut; I could not speak. I was speechless.

I *could* have said something to Anthony, like, "I'm not the one who eats beef jerky for breakfast," or "The only thing worse than that stench is your breath."

But I didn't say anything like that. All I did was sit there with my mouth hanging open. I felt just like a big-mouthed frog waiting for a fly to go zooming by so I could snatch him up with my frog tongue. I wished I *was* a big-mouthed frog sitting on a lily pad somewhere, waiting for a fly to go by. But I was not a big-mouthed frog. I was just, everyone else believed, the smelliest kid in fourth grade.

CHAPTER 2

I Heard He Threw Up

Lunch was, in a word, a nightmare. As I walked into the big, nasty cafeteria, I knew immediately that word had spread. You know how it is in the lunchroom. It's not just your class anymore. It is *all* the classes. In my case, it was four other fourth-grade classes. We are talking about one hundred fourth graders. We are talking about two hundred eyes all on me. We are talking about one hundred fingers on one hundred noses, and all in honor of me.

Don't ask me how word of the Anthony incident spread so fast. Things like this travel at the speed of light. They are whispered from kid to kid until they have been whispered in every ear. The story never stays the same, either. Kids always add in a little more detail just for excitement. I'm sure by now the story was that I smelled so bad that my desk caught fire. I bet by now the story probably was that the paint in my classroom actually melted off the walls. I bet...

Just as I was about to imagine another awful possibility, I felt a tug on my arm.

"It wasn't me!" I blurted out.

"Well, you're sure not acting like it, my friend," a voice replied. The voice and the tug came from my best friend, Scott. "Come on, let's get in line," he said.

It was Friday, pizza day. At least there was one thing I could be happy about. I followed Scott toward the line. All the while, I was aware of the eyes on me, the whispering that was going on all around me. Then it happened. A boy, whose name I don't even know from Mrs. Roth's class, said, "Here comes S.B.D.," as I walked by him and his friends at their lunch table. By the time I reached the line, which was long, kids started rushing back to their tables without any food. I heard it again, "Ew, it's S.B.D." I wasn't sure who said it.

"This is awesome!" Scott said. "The line is gone."

"This is not awesome," I replied, walking up to get our food.

"No line on pizza day is pretty awesome to me. When does that ever happen?" he said.

"Do you know why there isn't a line anymore on pizza day?" I asked in an annoyed voice.

"Yeah, you dropped a bomb at morning meeting in class today," he said as he selected the perfect chocolate milk.

"I did not drop a bomb at morning meeting," I said and picked out my own milk.

"That's not what I heard. I heard you really messed things up in there. I heard Mr. C. threw up in a garbage pail!"

"Are you kidding me? You really believe that I would do that in class? You really think Mr. C. threw up in a garbage pail?" I asked.

Mrs. Lamery, the lunch lady, must have been listening to our conversation, because from behind the lunch counter, she said, "I heard Mr. C. threw up on your shoes."

"No one threw up!" I shouted.

"Okay, take it easy. That'll be $1.25 please," she said with a smile.

"I heard he threw up," Scott said again.

"Errrrrr," I said.

CHAPTER 3

Why Do I Pay Attention?

After lunch, Mr. C. was going on and on about famous scientists and the importance of science. He said scientists cure diseases, discover new things and places, and try to make the world a better place. "Revolutionary thinkers" is what Mr. C. always calls them: people who think and discover things that no one before them ever did. He said we should try to think like great scientists when we plan for our science-fair projects. We had to come up with an idea for the science fair and submit it for approval by next week.

I was still pretty upset about taking the blame for Anthony. Lunch period had not been kind to me. Kids kept saying things like, "Maybe you should go see the nurse," and "Next time just head on down to the bathroom." And a few more times I was referred to as S.B.D. (which stands for silent but deadly).

Plus, Mr. C. is a little too into science if you ask me. He gets so into it sometimes that I don't really know what he's talking about. When he's going on about science, I'm pretty sure he forgets that we're only nine and ten years old. I think he looks out on our bored faces and sees interested scientists when most of us are just daydreaming about gym.

Some of the kids in my class can actually tune him out and think of other things. I can't. I hear every painful word he says. Sometimes I try to imagine that I'm playing *Tenlax: Return of the Mariner*, my favorite video game. I try to actually feel the controller in my hand. I try to envision the images on the screen and hear the sounds, but I always end up just listening to Mr. C. Sometimes I think I'm the only one listening to him because no one ever asks any questions or even looks up.

I usually make the mistake of looking up. My dad always taught me from the time I was real little to look a man in the eye when he's speaking to you. Now, I can't help it, even if I don't want to. It gets me in trouble because when Mr. C. takes a breath and looks around, I'm always the one looking back. He misinterprets this as me being interested and asks me questions.

Today, he asked me what I would change if I could change anything in the whole world. I didn't hesitate: "My seat."

Anthony turned around and stared right at me. I stared right back.

"S.B.D.," he said, and the class began to giggle.

Again, I said nothing.

CHAPTER 4

Living with the Machine

My dad even calls them S.B.D.s. My dad seems to have an endless list of ridiculous names for them, but S.B.D. is his favorite. I know you've experienced an S.B.D. We all have. You may have, as my dad says, "walked into one" at the mall, the hallway at school, or the supermarket. You know? You're walking along, minding your own business, and all of a sudden the air goes rancid and you want to just yak! You look around and try to figure out who did it. It's impossible to tell.

I have met only one person in my short, nine-year-long life who openly admits to stinking up a room, a person who seems to enjoy the torture he puts the rest of us through when he does it. When it happens—and it always happens—he just gets this big smile on his face and says something like "Oops" or "That one slipped out." The thing is, none of them ever "just slip out." He does it on purpose. I'm sure of it. The look on his face says it all. He doesn't look embarrassed; he looks proud.

And that person is none other than my dad! Some nights he drops one about every fifteen minutes, and they are something to behold. I call them D-bombs, and I've been on the receiving end of more than my share of D-bombs.

It happened like this. My family and I were watching TV, and at first I wasn't sure. Like I said, you know one minute everything is fine, and then the next your nose is sending SOS signals to your brain. I noticed the faces around me having the same stunned reaction as the kids in my class had earlier that day. My sister, who is only three years old, simply ran out of the room holding her nose. She just got up and shot out of the room without saying a single word, leaving her princess toys on the floor. My mother, who was reading a magazine, slowly set it down on her lap, tilted her head to one side, and looked in my direction.

"Keith? Was that you?" she asked. She always asks if it's me first. I don't know why because it's always my dad. Maybe she can't face the fact that she married a smelly monster of a man.

"No, it wasn't me!" I exclaimed.

"Are you sure?" she asked again.

"Mom, I'm nine. I am not capable of such horrible things," I said.

"I'm sorry," my dad began. "It must have just slipped out."

"Honey, that was really gross," my mom said, holding the magazine over her face to hide the awful stench. On the cover was a woman smiling on a beach somewhere. *Lady, if you could smell what I smell, you wouldn't be smiling*, I thought. *If you could smell what I smell, you would run out of here like my kid sister just did.*

"I know. It won't happen again," my dad promised.

I may only be nine, but I know enough not to believe that one. My dad always says it won't happen again, and he always lets it happen again. I decided it was a good time to go to bed.

"Good night, everybody. I'm out," I said abruptly.

"Give me a hug, pal," my dad said with a smirk on his face.

"How about I owe you one, Dad," I said.

"Suit yourself, sport. I'm just trying to show my son I love him," he said as I kissed Mom good night. "Come on, buddy boy. Give your dear old dad a hugsy."

"Good night, Dad. Maybe tomorrow."

As I said that, he leaned on his left side and put another one into the couch.

"Then again, maybe not," I said.

"Come on, bud. It slipped out!" he exclaimed through his laughter.

CHAPTER 5

Grandma

The next day was Saturday, and I woke up late. The clock next to my bed read ten fifteen. I never sleep past eight, because my sister Emma always comes running into my room to wake me up. I sat up and turned the plastic stick on my blinds. The bright sunlight immediately filled my room, and I felt very hot. I got out of bed and pushed the window open. A nice breeze came through the slots in the blinds. What a relief it was to have fresh air for a change. Yesterday really stunk. I was ready for a new day.

I love Saturdays, especially Saturdays when I have nothing to do and nowhere to be. I got dressed and left my room to see what I was missing. I couldn't believe how quiet it was. My house is never that quiet. Usually I hear my sister making all kinds of three-year-old noise: her toys that talk and giggle, her organ that has a microphone she loves to sing into, and her electric guitar that she plays by pressing buttons. But today there was none of that. It was silent.

As I slowly walked down the stairs, I heard sounds coming from the kitchen. My grandmother was cooking something on the stove and listening to the stereo. My grandmother is not your average grandmother. She likes to listen to the same music I listen to. She was listening to my CD of the Milkheads and singing along.

"Hi, Grandma," I said.

"Hey, Rock Star. You sure slept well last night."

"Yeah."

"Where is everybody?"

"Your mother took your sister to her friend Emily's birthday party at Fun Explosion. Your dad went with them. They were going to wake you up to go, but I figured you would rather sleep in."

"Thank you. Do you have any idea how annoying those parties are?"

"I'm not there, am I?"

"No, you're not. Thanks for saving me, Grandma."

She looked at me with disbelieving eyes. "Okay, but if you decide to tell me, I'm all ears," she said as she kissed me on the forehead. As good as my grandmother made me feel, I knew Monday was sure to bring a whole new batch of trouble at school.

CHAPTER 6

What to Do?
What to Do?

Sunday night, I couldn't sleep. I just lay there in bed thinking about what I would do for my science project. I wanted to do something amazing. This project had to shift the focus off of my S.B.D. reputation. It had to be something that everyone would be talking about. Something that would make people go, "Wow!" And, of course, it had to be something easy. Not that I was being lazy, which I was, but I've got a life, you know? I can't lock myself up in the basement and experiment for a month straight. I had just gotten *Death March Dread* for my game system. I wondered if Mr. C. would let me do an experiment using *Death March*

Dread. Maybe I could see how long I could play it until I had to stop.

Maybe I could see how many bags of Cheesy Nacho Chips I could eat before I would stop liking them. There's something strange about Cheesy Nacho Chips. I can't eat just one. And I can't stop eating them once I've started. I can be thinking, *Okay, just one more.* But then I always end up eating one more and then one more until my mom says something like, "Keith, you're making me sick. Put those away before you turn into an orange triangle." I know I'm not the only one who can't stop. Every time Cheesy Nacho Chips are at a party, they're always gone before any other chip. People are always picking at the little crumbs at the bottom of the bowl and hoping the host will fill it up again. When they are all gone, people move on to other chips, but there is only one Cheesy Nacho Chip.

Maybe I can experiment with what magical ingredient makes people eat Cheesy Nacho Chips nonstop. There must be some secret ingredient to be discovered. Mr. C. said to do the science project on something you know about, something you're already interested in, with the bonus that "If your experiment attempts to make something in the world better, it will earn extra points."

I would get better at *Death March Dread* if I played it for two days straight. I would have to stay home from school in the name of science. An experiment on video games was definitely the way to go! Cheesy Nachos are delicious, but video games are the best. I couldn't wait to tell Mr. C. the next day.

Monday, when I mentioned it to Mr. C., he had one word for the project: no.

He didn't feel that my getting better at *Death March Dread* would help the world. I made the argument that I would be able to help the military in the future with the skills I was learning today. He said I had to help the world in a positive way without using video games.

On Tuesday, I tried again. I couldn't get the idea of playing video games for school out of my head. He said no again.

He told me to find something in my life that bothered me, and then figure out a way to make it better. "Chances are, if it bothers you, it bothers other people. Make lemons from lemonade," he said.

Whatever that means.

Mr. C. told us that we would have to get his approval before we could actually do our experiment. Wednesday would be the first day for preapproved presentations.

Wednesday morning Maggie Mender went first, showing off her environmentally safe cleaning supplies that, I think, were just bottles of water with lemon juice squeezed into them to make them smell good. But Mr. C. loved it.

Then Peter Jameson presented his experiment for trying to breed bees that don't have stingers, which is totally lame because we all know his grandfather is a beekeeper and would do the work for him. And finally, Clara Nasbaum presented on making clothes from garbage. Both of which Mr. C. approved and seemed to love.

I couldn't understand why *Death March Dread* was being discriminated against. All Mr. C. said was scientists pay attention to their surroundings and that is what drives their experiments.

As I sat there feeling sorry for myself, I noticed Anthony lift. He acted like he was just leaning over to get a pencil from the floor, but there were no pencils on the floor. Before I could raise my hand to ask to go to the bathroom or to get a drink or anything that would save me from the certain nostril assault heading my way, it was too late. I got tagged again.

Anthony slowly turned around and looked right at me. He shook his head back and forth like he was saying no, like he couldn't believe it had just happened.

"It wasn't me, Anthony. Don't even try..." I began.

"That's disgusting, S.B.D.," he said and turned back around.

"It wasn't me and you know it," I shot back. I was proud of myself. I had actually stood up to him.

"Oh yeah, then why are you so red in the face? You're embarrassed. You need to see a doctor. Can't you control yourself? You're like an animal in a zoo. We all know it was you."

"It was not," I shot back. I was doing pretty well.

"Come on, Keith. You look so guilty. If I farted, I would say so. Everybody knows that. This time, though, it was you. Just admit it."

Mr. C. interrupted us. "Hey, guys, let's focus on the science fair."

"But, Mr. C.," I began.

"Keith, if you're not feeling well again, just go down and use the bathroom. We talked about this the other day."

"But it wasn't me." Now I was starting to get angry.

I looked around, but there were no friendly faces. Kids were moving their chairs away from me.

Anthony was turning me into a monster. This couldn't be happening...again.

CHAPTER 7

That Night

That night Mom had made vegetable lasagna for dinner. I don't really like veggie lasagna, as she likes to call it. I ate it, though. I picked out all the carrots and celery, and afterwards I went and played video games for a while. Then she said it was homework time. My only homework was to decide on a topic for my project. I sat at the kitchen counter and rocked back and forth on one of the high chairs. They aren't high chairs like for a baby. They are chairs that are high. It's tricky because the floor in the kitchen is slippery, and the chair can easily slip. I have never slipped, and I take great pride in this accomplishment.

My mom caught me rocking out of the corner of her eye from the living room. I always find it interesting how she watches TV, but I have to do my homework. Sometimes I watch TV from the kitchen because I can see the TV in the living room. She got up and came in.

"Don't rock on that chair!" she said in a tough tone.

"I..."

She walked over and stood next to me.

"You're going to fall and break your neck one day, you know!"

"I wish I would break my neck. Then I wouldn't have to work on this lame science project," I said.

"I don't know much about science, but I'll help."

"I have to pick a topic by tomorrow. It's already a day late because my idea keeps getting rejected. I've been thinking about it for almost a week, and I can't come up with anything else. Mr. C. says we should follow in the footsteps of the great thinkers. We should try to change something in the world for the better."

"Hmmm. Well, what do you want to change about the world?"

"I don't know. I'm nine. Things seem pretty good in the world, except for science."

I knew that Mom was about to give me some suggestions that I would not like, but it meant a lot that she was trying to help. So I waited for the ridiculous ideas that were about to come out of her mouth. She thought hard for a few minutes. She looked like she was solving the riddles of the universe.

"How about seeing if you can create a new fertilizer for my roses? We can try different things mixed together and see which one helps the roses grow better."

"No. I don't think soooo. Kinda boring."

"How about you make me *bigga*?" my sister piped in from below.

"How will I make you bigga?" I asked, looking down on her smiling face.

"You can stretch me out," she said and held her arms out wide.

"How?" I asked, giggling.

"Hang me by my ankles until I'm bigga," she shouted.

"Now that I like," I said rubbing my chin.

"Thank you for trying to help your brother, Emma dear, but I think you're just right the way you are," my mom said, pinching her on her plump, pink cheek.

"I like being hunged upside *downeee*," she said.

My little sister was obsessed with being hung upside down. I didn't realize I was that strong, but I could hold her up for a few seconds by the ankles. It was fun at first, but I was getting kind of tired of it. I did it for the first time about a week before. Now she asked me to do it all the time. She has taken to begging and whining until I give in. To make matters worse, my mom thinks it is the cutest thing she's ever seen.

"Take a break and hang your sister upside down. I'll go get the video camera," Mom suggested, running off to the living room. I heard her footsteps climbing the stairs to her bedroom.

I really didn't want to hang Emma upside down again, but if it would get me out of my homework for a little while, so be it. I got a good grip on her ankles and was ready to yank her up just as Mom returned with the camera.

"Okay, let me get it ready," she said. "Okay, go, but be careful. Don't lift her too high—just a few inches from the ground. Accidents happen, you know."

I slowly pulled up on Emma's ankles. She was laughing hysterically and facing the camera. Mom turned around the little screen on the camera so Emma could see herself, focusing in real close so

Emma could get a good look. She was laughing about as hard as I'd ever heard her laugh. My mom was laughing, too. I was just happy not to be working on my project.

My sister's laugh kept getting more and more intense. It was one of those deep belly laughs that, when you hear it, you can't help but crack up yourself. There we were, all in the kitchen, my sister hanging by her ankles and all of us cracking up, when *it* happened.

I quickly realized why my sister went from laughing hard to laughing harder than she had ever laughed before in her life. She was laughing so hard she couldn't breathe. She had dusted me.

"Dusted" is another term my father uses for farting. Emma's didn't make a sound. It just crept up into my nose like a thief in the night. I didn't see it coming. I could not believe it. I'd been called S.B.D. at school more times in the last few days than I could remember, and now my own three-year-old sister was farting right on me.

My sister was now laughing so hard that tears were streaming down her pink cheeks. I felt myself getting very angry, angrier than I have ever been in my life. I didn't know what to do.

Here I was holding my sister by the ankles so she could have a good time, and this was the thanks I got! I don't know if I was that mad at *her* or if it was because of Anthony and all the S.B.D. stuff at school, but this was the last straw. I did the only thing I could think of...

I let her go.

CHAPTER 8

Eureka!

The next day, I woke up so early the alarm clock hadn't even gone off. I was so rested because Mom sent me to bed at seven o'clock after I dropped Emma on her head. All night long, all I could do was think about my experiment. I was having nightmares about being the only one at the fair without a project. When all of a sudden, I opened my eyes and sat up in bed.

It was perfect! It was genius! I rushed over to my backpack and took out the assignment page. I read all the steps of the scientific method. It was perfect. I knew what my experiment would be.

I started typing it out on the computer so fast my fingers could hardly keep up. I filled out every section of the scientific method with ease. I had never been more excited about a school project in my life.

Scientific Method

1.   Question: *Can I discover something that people can eat that will make their gas/farts smell good?*

I wondered whether I could use the word *fart* in a science-fair project. I probably could because I know they use that word on TV, and if they use it on TV, it's usually okay to say. But then again, there are words on TV that are not okay to say so I decided to go with *gas* instead. It sounded more scientific anyway.

2.   Hypothesis: *I think I can create something that people can eat and it will make their gas smell good because people have already discovered things that make cars, bathrooms, and armpits smell good. It should be possible to make human gas smell good, too.*

This was great. I was on a roll.

3. ***Materials:*** *An assortment of pleasant-smelling things that can be eaten. Fruits, vegetables, herbs, flower petals.*

4. ***Procedure:*** *First, I will create a rubric from 1 to 4 that determines how offensive a person's gas is. The rubric will be like a score. A score of 1 will be the worst-smelling gas; a score of a 2 will be bad, but not the worst; 3 will be better, but not good; and 4 will be good. For a person to get a 4 the gas will have to actually smell good.*

I will need volunteers to be a part of the experiment. They will have to eat different mixtures that I create and help me to see if their gas smell improves. I will record my findings and create a chart that shows my results.

5. ***Results:***

I couldn't fill that in yet because I hadn't done the experiment. So I saved my work on my computer and printed out a copy to take to school.

I could smell bacon frying downstairs, which meant my mom was up. It also meant that I would have to leave for the bus in twenty minutes. I couldn't believe nearly two hours had passed since I sat down.

"That's what I'm here for, my boy. I would do anything for you. You know that, right?" She always says this to me. And when she does, she always gets a real serious look on her face to make sure I understand that she would do *anything* for me.

"I know, Grandma. You're the best."

"Yes, I am. I also made your favorite breakfast: eggs and salsa."

"Thanks."

"So how are things going, sweets? Everything okay at school?"

"Not exactly," I began.

"What's wrong?" she asked.

I love my grandma, but this was a touchy subject to talk about. She's really cool and all, but we are talking about farts here. I didn't want her calling the school if I told her my new nickname was S.B.D. and making things even worse for me. I could just imagine the announcement on the loudspeaker on Monday morning. "May I have your attention, Harborside Elementary School! Keith Emerson's grandmother just called, and it turns out that he did not, in fact, fart in class on Friday. Please do not call him S.B.D. anymore."

"I'm fine," I said.

I waited anxiously as my printer hummed out my brilliance. Looking in the mirror as I waited, I wondered if this was what Einstein felt like when he figured out that $E=MC^2$ thing or how the Cheesy Nacho Chip guy felt the day he got the cheese *just* right. This was clearly a turning point in my life. I was now a great thinker.

I would be remembered two hundred years from now! I would be long dead, of course, but all people would remember me for would be my inventions and discoveries. Statues of me would stand in major universities and science museums around the world. Children would be reading about me in textbooks in the future. Only, in the future, I imagined textbooks would be made out of edible paper, so the kids would read about me and then eat the pages. I think I'd like my page to be nacho-cheese flavored.

"Keith! The bus will be here in ten minutes. What are you doing up there?" my mom yelled.

I shook my head and saw my reflection in the mirror over my desk. My eyes focused, and I noticed something move under my blanket.

Emma was in love with hiding. It was one of her favorite things to do. The problem was she didn't realize that people could hear her when she was hiding. And every time she hid, she began to giggle. That, and she usually had a foot or hand or half of her body hanging out from her hiding place, and that gave her away, too.

This time, it was half of her head. I could see her blond hair against my dark green sheets.

"Hmmm...I wonder where Emma is?" I said.

Giggles.

"Maybe she's under my bed."

"Noooo, I'm *nawt!*" she shouted.

"Maybe she's in my closet," I said.

"Nooo, I'm nawt!"

"Maybe she's..."

"*Here I am!*" she announced.

She popped out from under the blankets and looked about as a happy as a person can.

"I didn't know you were under there," I said.

"I'm pretty tricky, huh?" she asked seriously.

"You sure are. And you know what?"

"What?"

"You gave me an idea for my science experiment."

"Are you going to hide?"

"No."

"Are you going to stretch me out?"

"No."

She pulled the covers over her head again.

"You can't find me."

She also didn't realize that when she hid and I was right in front of her, I still knew where she was hiding.

"Keith! What are you doing?" my mom shouted.

"I'm coming, Mom," I shouted back.

"Hmmm, where could Emma be?" I said, pretending to be confused.

"You'll never find me."

I pulled the covers off her really fast. "Gotcha!" I said. She was laughing like crazy.

As she laughed, I noticed the bump on her forehead from when I dropped her. I sat down on the bed next to her. "Emma," I started, "I'm really sorry I dropped you last night. I was just really mad that you dusted me."

"I know," she said. "I made a bad choice."

"I shouldn't have done that, though. It isn't nice to hurt other people. I could have really hurt you. Do you forgive me?"

"*Yeeeaaahhh*," she said. "Can you do it again?"

"Why would I do it again?"

"I liked it. *Pleeeaaase.*"

"Keith, the bus is pulling up," my mom shouted.

"Sorry, sweets, I have to go. How about later I hang you by your ankles again, but this time I won't let go?"

"Okay, and I won't make a bubble."

"That sounds great."

My mom insists that my sister call farts "bubbles." She thinks the word *fart* is offensive. I don't know why. Everyone at school uses it. For some reason she gets really upset, so when I talk to my sister or my mom, they are bubbles, or *bubs* for short. To everyone else in the world, they are just farts.

CHAPTER 9

Am I Really Doing This?

When I sat down in my seat on the bus, it hit me. It was one thing to come up with this science-fair idea; it was another to actually share it with Mr. C. and the class. What if they laughed at me? What was I thinking? Of course, they would laugh at me. They all thought I was the fart king of New York. All you had to do is mention the word *fart* and half the kids in my class would start to giggle.

As the bus made the slow, wide turn into the school entrance, I felt my adrenaline kick in. All of a sudden my heart began to race faster and faster. I could feel my face getting red and hot. The noises on the bus grew louder. I noticed I was chewing my fingernails, tapping my feet, and humming all at once. I was freaking out!

I don't remember getting off the bus. I don't remember walking into school or taking off my coat. Before I knew it, I was sitting on the cold, dusty floor with the rest of the kids when I heard Mr. C. say, "Okay, Keith, it's your turn. Have you decided on a project that will change the world for the better?"

A lump formed in my throat the size of the lump on Emma's forehead. My stomach was doing the twist. I felt like I might faint.

"I think I have, Mr. Cherub," I said.

"Well, come on up and tell us all about it," he said.

I took a deep breath and walked to the front of the room. A few kids whispered, "S.B.D.," under their breath but loud enough for everyone to hear.

"Come on, guys," Mr. C. said.

Some other kids held their noses when I walked by, but most of the class didn't even bother to look up. Many of them were still half asleep.

I cleared my throat and in a low voice said, "My project is about gasses."

"Can you be more specific?" Mr. C. replied.

"I want to experiment with different foods to see if I can make gasses smell better."

No one seemed to be onto me. This was good. The more they didn't follow what I was really saying, the better chance I had of Mr. C. taking my idea seriously.

"What sort of gasses?" he asked.

"Well, gas that…well, has an unpleasant odor," I whispered.

"Do you mean pollution?" Mr. C. blurted out.

"You could say that."

"Well what sort of gas pollution are you talking about? Is it exhaust?"

"You could say that, too."

"Do you mean the gas coming from the rear of a car?"

When Mr. C. said "*REAR*," I almost lost it.

"Yes, it comes out of the rear," I said, a smile beginning to creep across my face.

"Of a car?" he asked.

"Not exactly," I said.

"Keith, if you're not talking about gas that comes out of the rear of a car, then what are you talking about?"

At this point kids were beginning to pay attention. By the looks on their faces, they weren't onto me yet. They just thought I had no idea what I was talking about, and there's nothing more interesting in school than watching another kid fall apart in front of the class.

"Well then, what sort of pollution are you experimenting with?" Mr. C. asked, signs of frustration beginning to show on his face. He shook his head and widened his eyes. It was clear he thought I was clueless.

"You know, *gas.*"

"There are many types of gas, Keith. There is methane, hydrogen, carbon dioxide. Even oxygen is a gas." He was almost yelling at this point.

I noticed a few faces light up. Were they onto me? A few giggles broke out. Mr. C. tried to hold them back by demanding, "Stop laughing!"

It didn't work. The giggles had now become contagious. I felt adrenaline rushing back through my veins. My heart raced like I was falling out of an airplane. I took a deep breath to try to calm down. The class was clearly onto me. The excitement in the room was poised to break loose.

"How is this gas released into the atmosphere?" Mr. C. asked.

The class exploded with laughter.

"Class, please, Keith is trying to explain his project." Everyone was now wide-awake. There wasn't a sleepy eye in the room.

"How is it released into the atmosphere?" he repeated over the laughter.

"From the rear," I explained. Sarah Stanton was taking a sip from her water bottle and sprayed it onto the back of Jason Calino's neck. He didn't seem to care.

"Please, class, calm down! It is not polite to laugh while your peer tries to share his ideas. Keith, please be more specific. The rear of what?" He had to shout this because the class was now officially out of control.

"Well...*people*!" I shouted back.

Mr. C. didn't say anything. He just looked at me. Looked *at* me doesn't quite describe it well enough. He looked *through* me. Mr. C. stood up and marched over to the phone on the far wall. I knew he was calling the principal. I had never been to the principal's office in my life. I guess that was about to change.

CHAPTER 10

The Principal's Office

I had never been to the principal's office before. Part of me felt tough and the other felt like crying because I knew my mom would kill me when she found out. I also felt plain embarrassed. I should have known better than to present such a crazy idea to my teacher. I'd never seen him look so angry. He thought I was playing a joke. The class was absolutely out of control; they were laughing so hard there was no bringing them back. I only wish I could have been on the laughing side of things. I sure wasn't laughing now.

Mrs. Barcelona, the office secretary, said the principal, Mr. Michaels, was at a meeting and should be back any minute. I realized as I sat there in the office that I had never actually spoken with

Mr. M. before. I didn't really know him. The only thing I knew was that he could destroy me.

I could see him coming up the front walk. He was wearing the kind of sunglasses that detectives wore in the old detective shows. He took them off as he opened the front door and entered the school, and I could see him squinting to see who was in the chair next to Mrs. Barcelona. My heart was beating so hard I could feel it in my throat.

He gave me a death stare as he entered the office, then walked right past me and began whispering to Mrs. Barcelona. She looked like she was laughing or at least grinning, and for a second, I think he might have smiled, too. Then he made a serious face.

He waved his hand for me to follow him into the office. His office was full of wooden furniture. He collected antiques and kept many of them in his office. That's about the only thing I knew about him. I sat down in a really old-looking chair and took a deep breath.

"So, Keith Emerson, would you like to tell me a little about this prank you decided to pull in Mr. Cherub's class this morning?"

"It wasn't a prank, sir. I was being serious." I couldn't believe he knew my name.

"You weren't trying to embarrass your teacher or be a wise guy?"

"No, sir. Mr. Cherub told us to focus on something that we knew and to try to change the world for the better."

"And you decided to do a project on flatulence?"

"No, sir, it was going to be on S.B.D.s." I couldn't believe I had just said "S.B.D." to the principal.

"I'm sorry?"

"No, sir. I'm sorry."

He smiled.

"No, Keith, flatulence and S.B.D. are the same thing, assuming that we are talking about the same thing."

More amazing than the fact that I had just said S.B.D. to my principal was that my principal had just said S.B.D. to me! I was definitely going to faint.

"I'm not sure what we're talking about anymore," I said.

"Do you mean silent but deadly?" he asked.

It was just too much. I looked around to make sure I wasn't on one of those hidden-camera shows. I felt like a cheesy TV host was going to walk in and tell me this was all a practical joke. This could not be happening. Maybe I was still in bed and dreaming. I shook my head back and forth. No, I was awake.

"I guess…well…yes."

"Okay, at least we are talking about the same thing. What exactly do you want to try in your experiment?"

I spent the next ten minutes explaining to Mr. Michaels about Anthony, the kids in the class, and how I had been labeled S.B.D. Not only did he look like he was really listening, but he was even taking notes on a yellow sticky pad.

"Okay, I'm going to give this some thought, and I will get back to you later today or tomorrow," he said when I finished my story.

"You mean you might actually let me do it?"

"*Might* being the key word here. I think it's a strange idea, but it does seem to fit Mr. Cherub's criteria, and it seems like you really are interested in the, umm…subject."

"Thanks, sir," I said, a little amazed.

I stood up and walked out of the office. Scott was coming down the hall with his class. They all looked at me with that you're-in-so-much-trouble look that everyone gets when they go to the principal's office. Scott's eyes seemed like they might burst out of his head.

"What happened?" he mouthed.

"I'll tell you at lunch," I mouthed back.

Then I noticed my class coming down the hall behind his. They were all giving me the same look.

"Please get in line with the class, Mr. Emerson. You and I will talk later," Mr. Cherub said.

"Okay," I replied, getting in line. I realized I had a smile on my face. I couldn't remember the last time I was smiling like this in school. I had faced down the principal and lived to tell about it.

At lunch, I took a bite of the ham sandwich Mom packed me and immediately felt a tug on my shirt. It was Scott. "I can't believe this," he said.

"You can't believe what?" I said.

"I can't believe Mr. Cherub sent you to the office because you farted again in class."

"I didn't fart in class ever, and that isn't why I went to the principal," I said.

"Well then, why were you in the office?"

"I was in the office because of my science-fair project idea," I said.

"What are you doing?" he asked.

"I want to fix farts once and for all. I want to figure out a way to make them smell better."

"Are you crazy? Do you want to be known as S.B.D. for the rest of your life? Do you think someone is going to want to be Mrs. S.B.D. when you grow up?"

"I'm not going to be S.B.D. forever. Besides, if I can fix farts, there will be no such thing as an S.B.D."

"You're going to be S.B.D. for life for this."

"Maybe," I replied. "We'll see."

CHAPTER 11

The Green Light

When I came back from recess later the next day, I noticed a yellow note in my classroom mailbox.

You have the green light. I spoke with Mr. C., and your project is approved. Stop by my office.
Mr. Michaels.

Mr. C. noticed me reading the note and said, "Keith, head on down to the office. Mr. M. wants to see you." The class went, "*OOOOOhhhhh*," as if I was in trouble again. I just smiled and headed down to the office.

CHAPTER 12

Thank You, Benjamin Franklin

I sat in the large leather chair across from Mr. Michaels. He was finishing up his phone call, and held up a hand signaling me to hold on a minute. I didn't want it to seem like I was staring at him, so I looked around the office.

My eyes were immediately drawn to his computer screen. He was on a search screen and there were two words in the search box. The first was *Franklin*, and the second was *farts*. I was convinced I had fallen asleep and would soon wake up to the smell of my little sister dusting me again.

Instead, Mr. Michaels hung up the phone and said, "So I see you got my note."

I nodded.

He continued, "I'm not sure if you know this about me, but I happen to be a big fan of Benjamin Franklin."

I'd never met anyone who just happened to be a *big* fan of Benjamin Franklin. I know people who are fans of the Yankees or the Mets, but not Benjamin Franklin. That's like saying, "I'm a big fan of the guy on the news or the president of some faraway country." It just doesn't make sense.

"When you and I spoke yesterday, your idea seemed very familiar to me for some reason. I couldn't figure out why…and then it hit me on the way home. I remembered reading something by Franklin called 'A Letter to a Royal Academy.'"

I wasn't sure why Mr. Michaels was telling me all this. All I knew was that by the excitement in his voice, I didn't seem to be in any trouble. And somehow, it seemed I had Benjamin Franklin to thank for my good luck.

"Franklin wrote the letter in 1781 to the Royal Academy of Brussels," Mr. Michaels said.

Oh no, I was getting bored already.

He leaned back in his chair and continued, "Back in the eighteenth century, there were many contests that were provided by academies or colleges. The academies would put a question or challenge before the thinkers of the time. Franklin wrote this letter as a suggestion for a contest challenge. In the letter, Franklin writes..." He started reading from the computer screen:

"It is universally well known that in digesting our common food, there is created or produced in the bowels of human creatures a great quantity of wind.

"That permitting this air to escape and mix with the atmosphere, is usually offensive to the company, from the fetid smell that accompanies it.

"That all well-bred people therefore, to avoid giving such offence, forcibly restrain the efforts of nature to discharge that wind."

Here he stopped.

"Do you follow so far?" he asked.

"Not even a little bit," I said.

"Okay. What Franklin is saying in his letter is everyone has gas. Also, everyone knows that gas is smelly, and so they try very hard to hold it in so they do not offend other people."

"That makes sense," I said.

"The letter goes on: *Were it not for the odiously offensive smell accompanying such escapes, polite people would probably be under no more restraint in discharging such wind in company, than they are in spitting, or blowing their noses.*"

He stopped again. "Did you follow that?" he asked

"Umm...no," I said.

"He is saying that if gas did not smell bad, people would not be embarrassed to relieve themselves of it in public. It would be no worse than blowing your nose."

"Okay, I'm with you," I said.

He continued, "*My prize question therefore should be, to discover some drug wholesome and not disagreeable, to be mixed with our common food, or sauces, that shall render the natural discharges of wind from our bodies, not only inoffensive, but agreeable as perfumes.*"

"I understood perfume," I said.

"He's saying that his idea for the Royal Academy is to challenge someone to discover something that, when put in food, makes people's gas smell good."

"Hey, that's my idea."

"Exactly," he said. "And that is exactly why your project has been approved. As it turns out, your crazy idea, as strange as it may be, is going to attempt to solve a challenge that Benjamin Franklin put before the scientific community more than two hundred years ago."

All of a sudden, this went from being a silly science experiment idea to being something bigger. And I could see that Mr. M. was very excited.

"There's more," he said. "Franklin goes on to say:

"Let it be considered of how small importance to mankind, or to how small a part of mankind have been useful those discoveries in science that have heretofore made philosophers famous. Are there twenty men in Europe at this day, the happier, or even the easier, for any knowledge they have pick'd out of Aristotle? What comfort can the Vortices of

Descartes give to a man who has whirlwinds in his bowels! The knowledge of Newton's Mutual Attraction of the particles of matter, can it afford ease to him who is rack'd by their mutual repulsion.... Can it be compared with the ease and comfort every man living might feel seven times a day, by discharging freely the wind from his bowels? Especially if it be converted into a perfume.... And surely such a liberty of Expressing one's scent-iments, and pleasing one another, is of infinitely more importance to human happiness than that liberty of the press.... And I cannot but conclude, that in comparison therewith, for universal and continual utility, the science of the philosophers above-mentioned...are all together, scarcely worth a FART-hing."

After that, he laughed.

"I got a little bit of that," I said. Of course, I had no idea what he had just said.

"What did you get?"

"I got that he thinks this invention of better-smelling gas is important."

"More than important, he says that if someone can discover something to make the gas of people smell good, it would be the greatest discovery of all time. It would make most other discoveries seem worthless in comparison. He is saying that it would be *the* discovery of *all* discoveries!"

Now I was more than a little nervous; I was totally freaked out. I wasn't just doing a science experiment anymore; I was trying to solve a great challenge created by Benjamin Franklin!

"I don't think I can do it," I said.

"What do you mean?"

"This is all a little too much. I just wanted to do something familiar to me. I just wanted to fix something I thought was wrong with the world. I never expected it to turn into such a big deal."

"Well, it has turned into a big deal. And you're doing this experiment. I am officially assigning it to you. If you want to pass science this trimester, you are doing this experiment. This is your idea, and it's a great one. You should feel proud that you came up with the same idea that Benjamin Franklin did over two hundred years ago. You owe it to yourself, you owe it to me, and you owe it to Benjamin Franklin to do this science experiment.

"Who knows?" he said, leaning in closer to me. "Maybe you'll change the world."

CHAPTER 13

Now What?

So now I had the approval of Mr. M., my principal; Mr. C., my teacher; and strangely, Benjamin Franklin, great American scientist. Things had become a lot bigger than I had bargained for. Now came the real work. I had to decide what exactly I was going to test to try and make gas smell good.

I really could not believe what Franklin wrote. It was as if we knew each other. I would have figured someone like him would have only had incredible ideas, like discovering electricity. How in the world could someone so smart think of something so silly? I have to admit, it made me feel smarter to know I shared an idea with a great thinker, a revolutionary thinker.

Imagine if I could make something that makes people's gas smell like roses or cotton candy. Imagine if when you passed gas, you could do it out in public, and no one would think you were gross. Imagine if people actually complimented you on it...

"Nice fart, Keith. Can you make another one?"

It would be strange, but it would be an improvement. I decided the world was ready for new and improved farts.

Plus Mr. Cherub always said that even if a scientist is wrong, it's okay. The goal of science is to build knowledge and try new things. This certainly would be a new idea.

I thought to myself, *What smells really good? Roses do. People love the smell of roses. Maybe cotton candy? Popcorn would make a great scent. Bubble gum, cherries, oranges, anything at all would be better than what they smell like now. Heck, they could smell like cardboard, and that would be better.*

The toughest part of the experiment would be smelling people's farts in order to rate them. My whole life I had learned to run from farts, to get as far away as possible and not look back. Now I would have to go against everything my brain told me and stand my ground. I would have to smell my family's farts. I would have to take it like a man, in the name of science.

I sat my family down before dinner on Friday night and explained what I was planning on doing. My mother immediately said that she thought it was a bad idea. My father agreed with her but he had that look on his face like he wanted so badly to laugh but knew he couldn't. My sister just looked confused.

"I don't understand," my mom said. "How come you can't just do a project on volcanoes or make a tornado in a bottle like you did last year?"

"Because, Mom, this is real science. Those other experiments were kid's stuff. Besides, I'm trying to answer a challenge that Ben Franklin gave in 1781."

"What are you talking about?" my dad asked.

"I came up with the idea, and my teacher said no, and then I was sent to the principal, and he seemed really mad. But then, later, he called me back to his office and told me I had to do it because Benjamin Franklin had challenged scientists to do this same thing back in 1781, and no one had ever accomplished the challenge or maybe they didn't take it seriously but I am and..." I was rambling on and running out of breath.

"Wait a second!" my mom said. "Stop for just one second. Did you just say Benjamin Franklin had the idea to make gas smell good, too?"

"Yes."

"And your principal told you this?"

"Yes."

"And this letter was written by Benjamin Franklin?"

"Yes."

"Ben Franklin who discovered electricity and eyeglasses and the stove?"

"Yes."

"And he wants you to make farts smell good?"

"Well, yes."

"Are you serious?"

"Of *course* I'm serious, Mom."

"You expect me to believe that Ben Franklin wrote a letter about farting? And you want me to also believe that your principal is asking you to do a project on farts?"

My sister raised her hand. "Yes, Emma?" my mom said.

My sister smiled really big and said in a low voice, "We don't say *fawt* in this house."

My mother closed her eyes and took a deep breath. She was getting very frustrated.

I said, "He isn't asking anymore; he is telling me. He says I might be a great thinker."

"He is telling you this might make you a great thinker?"

"Mom?"

"Yes?"

"Why do you keep repeating everything I say?"

"Why do I keep repeating everything you say?"

"You did it again."

"I did it again? I did it *again*? I know I did it again. I keep repeating what you're saying because I can't believe what you are saying."

The next few seconds passed by very slowly. My mom and I just stared at each other. My father took his laptop out of his bag on the floor near the table and fired it up.

"He's telling the truth, Liz," my father said a moment later, breaking the silence.

On the screen was a copy of Ben Franklin's letter to the Royal Academy.

"That's it," I said.

My mom put her head in her hands and sighed. "The girls on the PTA are never going to let me live this one down."

I grinned. "I'm going to go down in history, Mom. Just you watch."

"That's what I'm afraid of," she sighed.

Rubric

1 = Lethal
2 = Toxic
3 = Fair
4 = Enjoyable/Pleasant

Dad		Emma	
Date	Score	Date	Score

CHAPTER 14
Trial Number One

Later that night, I created a list of things I thought might help make farts smell better.

My List
Rose petals
Daisies
Perfume on your food
Spoonful of sugar
Cotton candy
Herbs
Lemon zest
Soap flakes
Pollen
Baking soda
Baby powder

Lemon/lime/orange juice combination

I decided to do my first trial that night. Why wait around and worry about it? I would need to make my family stick to a strict diet. The foods they ate could not change. That way, the only thing changing would be the ingredient I decided to give them. I had one month until the science fair. I decided to pick three things to test: rose petals, baking soda, and a lemon/lime/orange juice combination. I would give each one to them for a week to see if there was any improvement in their gas smell.

Later on I sat them all down to explain my idea. "I am not going to do this," my mom began.

"But what about supporting your son?" I asked.

"There is something very important that you are forgetting, Keith," she said.

"What is that, Mom?"

"You are forgetting that I do not pass gas. A lady never does."

"Come on, Mom. You're going to tell me that you never pass gas?"

"Now *you* are the one repeating things," she said.

"Never once?"

"Never once," she said. My dad laughed.

"Don't you even say a word, Mr. Oops," she said. "Keith, listen to me very carefully. I do not pass gas, and I will not participate in your little farting contest. I will support you and help you in any way I can, but I will not be a part of this experiment."

"I want to be in a contest," my sister said. "Can I win a prize?"

"Not really," I said. "It's not that kind of a contest, Emma. It's not really a contest at all. I just want to see if I can make farts smell good."

"We do not say *fawts* in this house," my sister insisted. "We call them *bubs*. And bubs don't smell good. They smell *gwose*," she said scrunching up her face.

"I know. I'm trying to fix them so they smell good."

"Your sister and I would be happy to help," my dad said.

"Okay, good. The first thing we have to decide on is your diet. You are going to have to eat the same thing every day for a month. We can't change your diet in any way because it could alter the experiment."

"I want to eat cookies," my sister said.

"Me, too," my dad added.

"I don't think so," my mom replied. "I'll make you guys chicken cutlets, rice, and a salad every night."

"I don't want salad and chicken. I want cookies," my sister whined.

"You can't eat only cookies for a month," my mom said.

"I want cookies and ice cream then."

"You are going to have chicken because it is good for you. You will also have rice and a salad. And if you eat all of those every night, I will make you cookies. Is that fair?"

"Okay, but I only want the cookies. I do not have to eat the chicken."

"Emma, do you want to be in your brother's experiment or not?"

"I do want *toooo*," she begged.

"Okay, then you will eat what Mommy makes for you."

"*Awlwight*," she agreed.

I cleared my throat. "We will also have to include one other thing for you to eat. I'll have you eat each item for a week, along with the rest of your diet. I'll keep track of any improvements by following my rubric. For the first week, though, I will have you eat only what Mom makes you so I can get an accurate idea of how bad your bubs really are. We won't add anything to your diet that might improve the smell of your gas until next week."

"When would you like to start?" my dad asked.

"How about tonight?" I said.

After dinner, I went in my room to play video games. I had just sat down at the computer when my sister burst in.

"I'm ready," she said.

"You're ready for what?" I said.

"I'm ready to make a bub for you."

"Okay," I said. "Wait, don't do it yet. Let me get my clipboard with my rubric." As I went to get my clipboard, I started to feel a little sick. Was I really going to let my little sister fart and then smell it on purpose? I realized at that moment what Franklin was talking about when he said it would be the discovery of all discoveries. The person doing the experiment would have to smell farts until he found a cure. I quickly decided it was worth it to smell a lot of farts in a few weeks if that meant I would possibly never have to smell them again.

"Okay, let it rip," I told my sister. I waited, holding my pencil and my clipboard, bracing myself for the worst. It was like waiting for someone to pinch you. I just wanted to run. But I didn't, and she didn't, either. We both just stared at each other for a few seconds.

"I can't," she said finally and put her head down.

"Why not?" I asked.

"I think I am afraid." Then she started to cry. "Mommy, I can't make a bubble. I can't make a bubble," she yelled and ran out of my room crying.

I sat there shaking my head, wondering what I had gotten myself into. I could have done a volcano, and I'd be done by now. I could have made a tornado in a bottle, and I would have been done in the time it takes to fill a two-liter soda bottle with water.

The next thing I knew, my dad appeared in my doorway.

"I am reporting for duty. And I am afraid you may be the next one to run out of here in tears."

"Oh no…" I said.

"Oh no, indeed," he said. "Oh no, indeed, son."

CHAPTER 15

What Did You Tell Her?

Saturday morning I woke up and felt like I hadn't slept at all. You know those days when you wake up having the same thoughts you had the night before? This was one of those mornings. I had fallen asleep thinking about my project, and now I was waking up thinking about my project. I couldn't help it. Not only was the principal excited about what I was doing, but I was trying to live up to a challenge given by Benjamin Franklin over two hundred years ago and…then something struck me.

I realized that my house was quiet again. It was the same as last Saturday. I knew that my parents had to run to the hardware store to get paint for their room. I didn't think they would have left without me. They never left me home alone. I looked at my clock, which I couldn't see at all without my glasses. I felt around for my glasses on my nightstand. Once I got them on, I saw that it was already ten.

"Wow," I said out loud, breaking the silence.

"Wow is right," a voice shot back at me. It was Scott, and he was sitting at my desk, reading comics online.

"What are you doing here?" I asked, surprised.

"What are *you* doing here is the real question," he said. "We have a baseball game in twenty minutes and you're sleeping the day away."

"Well, I have a question for you," I said. "Why were you just sitting there? Why didn't you wake me up? Where's my family?"

"That's actually three questions. First, I was sitting here reading your notes from your science project. You happen to be very strange, you know. Second, I didn't wake you up because I don't have computer comics, and I am catching up. Third, your family left. They said you are too weird to be around now that you are a full-time fart sniffer."

"Very funny. Where is everyone?" I said as I got together my baseball stuff.

"Your grandma is in the yard with Emma. She told me to come and wake you up. She was asking me a whole lot of questions about what is going on with you at school."

"What do you mean? What did you tell her?"

"Nothing. I just told her that everyone in our school calls you S.B.D. now."

"What are you talking about? Why would you tell my grandmother that?"

"She gave me a whole bunch of cookies, and I was all pumped up on sugar. I just didn't think, I guess," he said as he read my online comics.

I went into the bathroom to get dressed for baseball. I stood there looking in the mirror for moment. *What am I going to tell Grandma? What am I going to do on science-fair night when I have to present this project to the class?* Then it hit me. My heart began to race. My palms got all sweaty. I took a deep breath. We were playing Anthony Papas's team in baseball.

CHAPTER 16

Hear Ye! Hear Ye!

Baseball is usually the highlight of my week, especially when the weather is just right. And the weather was just right. I didn't even need a jacket or a sweatshirt. I was crammed next to Scott and Emma in the backseat of Grandma's car, staring out the window at the town passing by.

"Why didn't you tell me you've been having gas problems?" Grandma asked from the front seat.

"I haven't been having gas problems," I said, feeling my cheeks brighten up with embarrassment.

"It's okay, sweets. It happens to all of us. The other day at the supermarket, I let one go waiting to check out. What can you do?"

"Mommy says a lady never makes bubs," Emma chimed in.

"Your mom may be an exception. But as far as I know everyone makes bubs," she said.

"What is a bub?" Scott asked.

"A fart," my sister blurted out.

"Emma," I said, "you know Mom doesn't like that word."

"What word?" Scott asked.

"*Fart*," I said.

"Why?"

"She just doesn't."

"She must really love your science-fair project, then."

"What is your science-fair project, Keith?" Grandma asked.

"Thanks, Scott. I wasn't exactly going to broadcast it to everyone."

"He's trying to discover a way to make farts, I mean bubs, smell good," Scott replied.

"Hmmmm," Grandma said with a smile.

"I want mine to smell like pickles," Emma said.

"I would want mine to smell like pizza. I love the smell of pizza," Scott said.

"I'd like mine to smell like orchids," Grandma said.

"I'm not taking requests, you know. I'm just trying to make them not smell bad, which is ridiculous. I'm pretty sure Mr. C. is hoping to make a fool of me with this."

"I'm not so sure. He seems pretty excited based on that interview he did with the paper," Scott said.

"What paper? What are you talking about?" I exclaimed.

"The *Daily*. It was in this morning's edition. It was like a half a page long. There was a picture of you and a picture of Benjamin Franklin right next to each other. They used your second-grade picture, I think. Remember the one where you're half smiling, half grimacing, like you stubbed your toe?"

"What are you talking about? They were talking about my project in the *Daily*? Why didn't they interview *me*?"

"I don't know. Mr. C. and Mr. Michaels were both interviewed. Mr. Michaels was going on and on, saying it could be the greatest discovery in science if you can pull it off. He's a really big Benjamin Franklin fan, you know."

"I'm aware. I'm aware," I said, staring out the window again.

CHAPTER 17

Fame and Shame

Walking up to the field, I noticed something unusual. It felt like everyone was staring at me. I put my bat behind the dugout and sat on the bench next to Scott. Grandma gave me a kiss on the top of the head and told me she'd be at the swings with Emma. Coach Willie walked up to me and slapped me on the back really hard.

"Looks like you're famous, gas man. Why didn't you ever tell me you were a science brain?"

"I'm not. I'm..." I began.

"I think it's great. Just try not to let it go to your head. All this attention could get to a guy."

"Okay, Coach," I said.

I looked across the field, and there was Anthony. This was just what I needed. I felt like crawling under the bench and just lying there until everyone had left. But I was our leadoff batter so I put on my batting helmet and walked up to the plate. The first pitch sailed by me for strike one. I wasn't sure if I was imagining it, but I thought I could hear the other team making noises. The second pitch sailed by for strike two. Yes, they were definitely making a noise. I couldn't make out what it was though. Strike three. As I was walking back to the dugout, it became clear. They were all making low farting noises. Anthony was laughing so hard, I could hear him all the way from left field.

The game went on pretty much like that until the bottom of the seventh. I was pitching now because Harry G. walked three batters in a row. The coach almost never let me pitch unless the other pitchers were doing terrible. Usually, I loved the opportunity to pitch, but today I didn't want to get any more attention than I already had.

That didn't matter much to Coach, though, and he stuck me on the mound. I threw a few warm-up pitches and signaled to the ump that I was ready. The other team was all seated. I should have known that Anthony would be the next guy up. He already had his helmet on. He walked up to the plate, making a farting noise every time he took a step. His teammates all made the same noise. Even one of their coaches got in on the action. Anthony had a huge smile on his face, and then he started laughing so hard he couldn't even swing at the first pitch. The second pitch went right on by, too, and then he stepped out of the batter's box, waving his hands to encourage his teammates to make the noise louder. Then he held his nose and pointed at me.

It was mortifying. I felt myself filling up with anger again, just like the night with Emma. I noticed Grandma was standing behind the dugout, watching all of this. I couldn't even lift my head. I was so embarrassed. For a minute, I thought I was going to cry.

Finally, a mother on the other team stood up and shouted, "That's enough! Everyone stop it and finish this game."

The other team stopped. They were still smiling, but at least they had stopped. It was dead quiet; you could have heard a pin drop. Even the wind had stopped. I just stood there, frozen, in some kind of shock or something. I didn't step to the pitcher's mound. I didn't look up. I just stood there looking at the ground. I was definitely going to cry. I could feel the tears starting to build up. I swallowed hard, trying to hold it back.

Then it happened. A loud fart cracked the silence like a whip. It seemed to echo across the field, the sound hanging in the air for what seemed like forever. I looked up, and all the eyes that had been locked on me all game long had shifted. Now they were all locked squarely on Grandma.

CHAPTER 18

What Were You Thinking?

On the ride home, no one said anything for a long time. Grandma, Scott, Emma, and I just sat silently as Grandma drove. Finally, I couldn't hold it in anymore.

"What were you thinking?" I groaned.

"I was trying to take all that terrible attention off of you, sweetie," she said with a smile.

"You couldn't think of any better way? I'm already known at school as S.B.D., and now my grandma drops a grandbomb at the game. This is going to ruin me."

"I think you're overreacting. This is a good thing for you. Now they will talk about me and not you. I'll be S.B.D. from now on. What do you say?"

"That's awesome," Scott said.

"No, it is not awesome," I shot back.

"Sure it is. She just saved you, Keith."

"Keith, I always told you I'd do anything for you. If that means publicly making a bub in order to save you from those mean boys, then bubs away, my boy."

"That's *so* awesome," Scott said, laughing.

I just looked out the window.

CHAPTER 19

Uncle

By the time we got home from the game, it was already twelve thirty. Mom and Dad were both back from the store. They were standing in front of the house, looking at the flowers. Dad had the lawnmower out for the first time this year.

"How was the game, bud?" he asked as I walked toward the front door.

I ignored him and ran up to my room. I threw myself onto the bed and started crying. This science fair was ruining my life. In the past week, I had been nicknamed S.B.D., sent to the principal's office, dropped my sister on her head, and been embarrassed in front of my whole baseball team. Now my own grandmother had joined me in the S.B.D. club.

My dad slowly opened the door. "Hey, what is going on with you? Grandma said you had an interesting game today." He walked over and sat on my bed, and then after a moment added, "Your grandma was just trying to help in her own bizarre way, you know? I didn't realize you were having so much trouble with the other kids. I wish you would have told us so we could have tried to help you deal with it."

"I know, Dad. I'm sorry. I've just had a bad week. At school, everyone thought I farted in class, and now they call me S.B.D. I'm the laughingstock of the fourth grade.

"And then I came up with this crazy idea to fix farts, and now my principal is making me do it and telling the whole town about it."

"I know how you feel, pal," Dad said. "Sometimes things don't go our way. We just have to keep on going. Before you know it, you will have survived it, and life will get better."

"Thanks, Dad. I know things will get better. I just can't take this project, and I can't handle Anthony Papas."

"Son."

"Yes, Dad?"

"Since we're talking about things you are not enjoying, I think you might want to take out your clipboard."

I just buried my head in my pillow. "Give me a second," I said.

"I think we're looking at a one on that rubric of yours, pal," he said.

"That sounds about right the way my day's been going."

CHAPTER 20
Not So Easy

By the end of the third week of my experiment, and the science fair less than two weeks away, I realized I was in trouble. I had tried my two best hypotheses on my sister and my dad. I sprinkled rose petals on their food for the entire second week. It did nothing. The third week, I gave them each a spoonful of baking soda because people say baking soda absorbs smells. I can tell you, it did not absorb the smell of my dad one bit. I sat at my desk, reviewing my data from the last three weeks. I had page after page of ones and twos on my rubrics. Neither of them ever came close to a three or a four.

My sister walked into my room and announced, "I'm ready to bub for you now."

"Great," I said sarcastically.

"Maybe this one will smell good, Keith," she said, looking at me with the most hopeful eyes.

"I doubt it," I said.

"I think it will smell like pickles," she whispered, as if it were a secret.

"You didn't even eat pickles today," I reminded her, smiling. As frustrated as I was feeling, I couldn't help but feel happy around her. My sister is about as cute as a person can be.

"I know, but I have been *thinking* about pickles all day," she said. Then she rubbed her chin very slowly with her right hand as if she were a detective. The cartoon cat in her favorite show does the same thing when he is trying to solve a mystery.

"Do you really think a pickle-smelling fart is any better than a regular old fart?" I asked.

"I like pickles. And Mom says not to say *fawt*."

"Well, if I ever figure out how to fix bubs, I'll make a pickle one for you."

"Here it comes," she said. I waited a minute. Her face became as red as an apple as she tried to force one out. Then a tiny squeak disrupted the silence.

"That definitely does not smell like pickles," I said.

After Emma left my room and went to bed, I began to look more closely at my dad's data. His seemed to be getting worse. Or maybe it was just that I had smelled so many of them in the last couple of weeks. My dad was enjoying this way too much. He had always been a farter, but now he acted like *I* was so fortunate he farted a lot.

A few minutes later I heard his footsteps on the stairs.

"I'm ready and willing to help in the name of science," he announced, standing in my doorway.

"Great," I said, without looking up.

"I'm afraid this one is not going to be what you're hoping for, pal."

"Well, let's just get it over with," I groaned.

"I tried to warn you. I think we're looking at another *uno* on that fart chart of yours."

CHAPTER 21

Defeat

The next week was pretty much the same. I added a mixture of lemon, lime, and orange juice to my family's food at every meal. My sister and my father came by my room a few times a day and stunk it up pretty good. I never once put a three or a four on the chart. Their farts kept on smelling like farts no matter what I did to improve them. Farts are farts, I finally decided. You can't fix them. It's just the way it is.

As I sat at my desk writing up my conclusion, I felt humiliated and embarrassed. What was I thinking? The kids at school would never stop giving me a hard time about this. Scott was right; I'd be S.B.D. for life.

The science fair was going to be a huge disappointment. Next year, I was definitely going to do a tornado in a bottle.

My conclusion was clear. I could not create a mixture that helped defeat the awful smell of farts even a little bit. The only good thing about the whole mess was that it didn't take me long to type up all the information on the computer. Most of the work was already done. I spent the rest of the night gluing my charts and pictures to my science board.

My title was:

"Farts, New and Improved?"

I was embarrassed about that, too, but that was the title I had submitted to Mr. C. when my project was approved, and he was making me stick with it.

After I finished pasting everything on the board, I stepped back to take the whole thing in. It didn't look very good. I wished I could carry it into the yard and throw it in the garbage. *I am definitely going to be made fun of when I bring this to school tomorrow*, I thought.

Farts:
New and Improved
by
Keith Emerson
Harbor Side Elementary

Results
I found that I could not improve Emma and Dads gas. Everytime I rated them it was a 1 or 2 on my rubric.

Problem / Purpose
I want to see if I can discover something that will make human gas smell good.

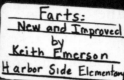

Data

Rubric
1 Lethal
2 Toxic
3 Fair
4 Enjoyable

DAD		EMMA	
3/2	1	3/2	2
3/3	1	3/3	2
3/4	2	3/4	1
3/5	1	3/5	1

Hypothesis
I think I can include rose petals, baking soda or a citrus mixture to a persons diet and improve the smell of their gas.

Conclusions
My hypothesis was incorrect. I could not discover anything that improved human gas.

Procedure
I had my sister and Dad eat the same diet for a month. I added one item each week hoping it would improve the smell of Emma and Dads gas.

Recommendations
I think that if I had more time I might have discovered something to improve human gas.

Procedure Cont'd
I created a rubric to rate the smell of their gas. I recorded results using a T-chart

CHAPTER 22

The Science Fair

The science fair was that night, and I realized there was only one thing to do: fake being sick.

"Mom, I can't go to the science fair. Maybe you could just go and pick up my project."

"Don't even try it. You are going to get dressed and go to that science fair. You can't just hide because you didn't get the results you wanted."

"Mom, I don't want to be laughed at."

"Neither did I when you told me about this crazy idea, but I stuck with it anyway. You don't think my friends find this whole thing funny? I think you need to decide if you are proud of what you tried to do. And I think you should be proud because you came up with the idea, a strange idea, but you came up with the idea nevertheless and you stuck with it. I think that's pretty great."

"Yeah, but the experiment proved nothing. I couldn't do anything that I wanted to do."

"Didn't you tell me that even when scientists fail, they are contributing to science? Maybe you didn't find the mixture you were looking for. Some scientists spend their entire lives trying to prove one hypothesis."

"I am definitely not going to spend my life letting people fart on me so I can write a number one or two on a chart. No way. From now on, I will be running from farts like the rest of the world."

"Well, I wish you would stop using that word, but I can't say I blame you. Come on. Let's go."

CHAPTER 23

Unfair Fair

I wanted to get to the fair early because a lot of kids can't get there until after their parents get home from work. I was the first one in the door. I walked around the school building trying to take my mind off the fact that my project would be laughed at all night. I tried to prepare myself.

As I walked around, I saw lots of volcanoes and tornadoes in a bottle, and something happened. I realized no one else had done anything like my project. I mean, anybody can look up a project on the computer and copy the directions. I had come up with a unique idea and tried to discover something new. Who cared if people made fun of it!

Of all the projects I saw, my favorite was the kid in third grade who mummified a twenty-five-pound turkey. The turkey was wrapped like a mummy and was sitting there all wrapped up. It had been wrapped over four months ago, and it didn't stink one bit. I couldn't say the same for my project.

When I finally went into my classroom, I could hear the laughter from the hallway.

"This project really stinks," Anthony cried. "The kid who did this project is really into farts. He farts all the time in class. I don't get people who fart. It is the grossest thing in the world." He was talking to a bunch of younger kids.

I couldn't believe that he was doing this to me.

I walked up to defend myself.

"Anthony, stop saying that about me."

As soon as I got close to him, I realized I was walking into a trap. Anthony had a great big smile on his face, and the other kids were holding their noses. He saw me coming and had dropped an A-bomb. I walked right into it.

"What did I tell you? The kid is a regular Pig-Pen."

"You stink, kid," one of the kids said.

"Whatever, your project was probably a tornado in a bottle," I replied.

"Actually, I mummified a turkey, and it doesn't stink!" he said. And they all walked away laughing. Again, I just stood there; I could not think of a thing to say.

CHAPTER 24

Mr. Gonzalez

After a while of feeling sorry for myself and listening to people make rude comments about my project, I noticed that I was all alone at my table, finally. I guess everyone thought that it stunk to be near me. I had heard every insult in the book. I couldn't wait for my mom to come back and pick me up.

I walked over to my desk and put my head down. It had been a long month. I had smelled about a thousand farts, been blamed for three S.B.D.s that were not mine, and was now the laughingstock of the lamest science fair ever. I must have closed my eyes for a few minutes, because when I opened them there was a man in a business suit standing in front of my presentation board.

He wasn't laughing, and he didn't seem shocked like most of the people who stopped to read it. He looked genuinely interested.

Mr. C. walked over and began to talk with him. I figured the man must be important because Mr. C. was acting very excited.

Mr. Cherub looked over at me and pointed; his hands were moving all over the place as if he were telling this great big story. Finally he waved me over.

"Keith, this is Mr. Gonzalez. He is the head of the Brookings Regional Science Center."

"Oh, hi. I'm Keith Emerson," I mumbled.

"I know. I read the article about you in the *Daily* a few weeks back. Your principal told me all about you and your project, but I'd love to hear about it from you."

Mr. C. excused himself and walked over to talk to a few parents who had wandered in.

"I came up with my idea because I seemed to be smelling other people's gas everywhere we went. My sister, my father, and this kid in my class were passing gas all the time. I finally got sick of it and tried to fix the problem once and for all. You know, if life gives you lemons, make lemonade."

"I know," Mr. Gonzalez said.

"Unfortunately, it didn't work out. I couldn't come up with anything that worked even a little bit."

"Well, that is unfortunate, but it's not a total loss."

"What do you mean?"

"Well, when I heard about your idea, I decided to come and meet you and ask you a question."

"What? You don't want me to rate your gas, do you? Because I can tell you from experience, you're probably a one or a two. We all are."

He gave me a funny look. "No, of course not, I wanted to ask your permission to continue your experiment at the lab. We want to try some ideas of our own but also try to prove your hypothesis."

"Really?"

"Really. We want to make sure it's okay with you and want to include you in the research and testing."

"You want me to rate the farts, don't you?"

"Well, we want you to work with us. You won't have to rate the, umm, farts anymore, though. If we are successful, we will, of course, share the profits with you."

"Of course," I found myself saying, as if I knew what the word *profit* actually meant.

"Are your parents here? I'd like to let them know what we have been talking about and make sure they support the idea."

"You don't have to worry about that. This was the best thing that ever happened to my dad. He will be thrilled that it's not over."

CHAPTER 25

Thank You, Everyone

I'm happy to report that after several months of working with Mr. Gonzalez and his scientists, we *finally* did it. We created little tablets that interact with gasses in the intestines and change the bad smell of farts to a good smell. We named the tablets Sweet Farts.

Soon after the discovery, we attended a conference in New York City. I met Mr. Gonzalez and his staff for lunch at this very fancy restaurant. My mom and dad were all dressed up, and my grandma was smiling from ear to ear.

They all seemed so proud to be with me. We sat at a table together and talked about all the crazy things that had happened to us since I first thought of the idea for the experiment.

After lunch, the conference began with a few people presenting their research findings on different topics. There were experiments on pollution, training dolphins to speak, and hair growth medicine for men. Then they announced us.

Mr. Gonzalez went up on stage to introduce our research. "Today I am before you to share our recent findings in the science of human gas. I am proud to say that the idea for this experiment came from a nine-year-old boy and his desire to, in his words, 'change something in the world that he didn't like.' I am confident that after we share our findings, you will agree that he has done more than that.

"Interestingly, this young boy's idea happened to be an idea that was first introduced to the scientific community in 1781 by none other than Mr. Benjamin Franklin. Although Franklin presented it as a joke, I'm sure that if he were here today, he would share in our enthusiasm. To paraphrase Franklin's words, 'The person who can cure the odor of human gas is greater than all the thinkers and all the great discoveries of the past combined.' Well, distinguished colleagues, friends, today I present to you—at least according to Mr.

Benjamin Franklin—the greatest scientific mind of all time, Keith Emerson."

I wasn't exactly sure what to do. There was a spotlight on me, and everyone in the room was looking at me and clapping. Mr. Gonzalez signaled for me to join him on stage.

I climbed the steps to the stage nervously and slowly approached Mr. Gonzalez and the podium. He moved back from the microphone and pointed for me to walk up to it. Slowly I approached the microphone. I heard my sister yell, "Hi, Keith! He's my big *brothow*!"

"Hi, Emma," I called back.

Then a man in the front row cried out, "Tell us about your experiment."

I looked at Mr. Gonzalez and then at my mom, dad, and grandma, and then I began to tell the story. I told them all about my dad, and my sister, and Anthony. I told them about how I was picked on and principal's office and the letter Franklin wrote. I told them about my grandmother fulfilling her promise to do anything for me. (She even got a standing ovation and took a big bow.) I told them how my project failed to find a cure for gas. And then finally I told them about Mr. Gonzalez and the laboratory.

People began to clap, and I felt really good. My family was smiling, and everyone was really interested in me and my crazy experiment. Then something funny happened. My idea didn't seem so crazy anymore. Mr. Gonzalez came back up to the microphone and handed me a packet of Sweet Farts. I began to explain to everyone in the room that we had in fact discovered a cure for bad gas. While Mr. Gonzalez had a few of his assistants hand out the packets to everyone in the audience, I explained how they worked.

"Basically, after you eat this tablet, it reacts with the gasses in your intestines and changes the gas smell to the smell in the tablets."

People began raising their hands. I called on the first person I saw.

"Have you tested it? Do you know that it works?"

I looked at my dad and smiled. "Yes, we have tested it many times, and I can assure you it works."

My sister shouted out from her seat, "I helped."

"Yes," I said. "My sister and my father were of great help. My mom did not help because she does not pass gas." Everyone laughed.

"What scents have you developed?" a woman with a microphone asked.

"We have summer rose, cotton candy, grape, and pickles."

"Did you say pickles?"

"Ask my sister," I said.

"I like pickles," my sister called out. "Keith promised me that he would make that scent just for me."

"This is all very interesting, but do you think people even want to change the smell of their gas?" a man in the audience asked.

"Well, I think so, yes. I mean, if you could never smell bad gas again in your life, wouldn't that be something you'd want?"

"Well, I guess so," he said.

"It takes a while to get used to the idea of gas that doesn't smell bad, but I think it will be nice for people to not have to feel ashamed of something that is perfectly natural and happens seven or more times per day to all of us. I think in five years, farting won't be any more embarrassing than blowing your nose— that is, if everyone starts taking our Sweet Fart tablets."

Everyone applauded. I walked off the stage, and my family was waiting for me with Mr. Gonzalez. I couldn't believe this was all happening. And as it turned out, this was only the beginning.

CHAPTER 26

The Very Next Morning

The very next morning, the Sweet Farts packets went on sale around the whole country. We were planning to go to the Browse and Buy Supermarket and pick up a few packs just for fun.

My mom woke me up at eight o'clock, even though it was a Sunday. "Keith, get up. You have got to see this."

She turned on my TV, something she never does first thing in the morning (she says it rots your brain).

The first channel she landed on was one of those news channels. They were talking about Sweet Farts. I couldn't believe it. She turned the channel, and that channel was talking about Sweet Farts. She kept on flipping, and they were all talking about the same thing. One of the shows even had my picture on the screen. Another had Mr. Gonzalez talking to one of the interviewers. I felt like I was dreaming.

Suddenly there was a lot of noise outside my window. My mom walked over and pulled up the shade to see what was happening.

"Oh my gosh!"

"What is it, Mom?"

"You have to come and see for yourself."

I walked over and saw vans and satellite dishes and reporters up and down our street. There must have been fifty vans and a hundred reporters. They were all in front of our house. My mom and I looked at each other.

"What do we do now?" I asked her.

"I guess we get you dressed and go out and see what they want."

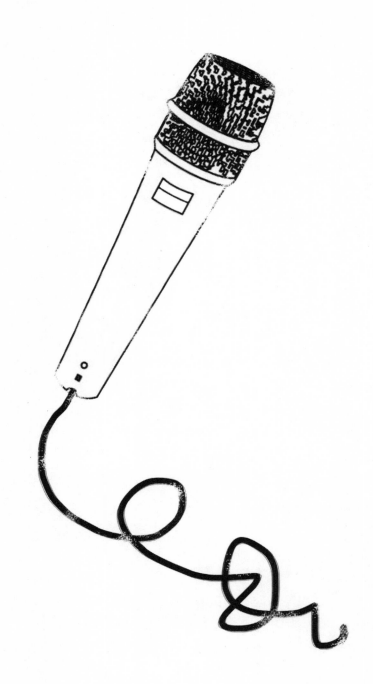

CHAPTER 27

That Was Me, Everybody

My whole family got dressed in record time. When we opened the door, there was a tidal wave of reporters running up the path to the front door. When they reached the door, they shoved microphones in our faces.

"Hold on a second," my dad said. "Everyone calm down and I'll let you ask your questions."

A voice behind one of the microphones asked, "How do you feel about all this?"

"I don't know," I said. "I just woke up."

The questions just kept coming. I must have answered a thousand questions that morning. I was starting to get tired when something didn't seem right. First, I got a whiff and then the full smell hit my nose. Everyone else must have smelled it, too, from the looks on their faces. But instead of looks of disgust, everyone was smiling. It was not that strong at first, but then it grew stronger and stronger. It smelled like grapes.

"That was me," admitted one of the reporters. Everyone laughed.

"Hey, this stuff really works, huh, kid?"

"It sure does," I said.

"Thank you," another voice from the crowd chimed in.

"Yeah, thank you!" said another. Then something strange happened. All the reporters began to clap and cheer. I guess I wasn't the only person who was tired of smelling bad gas.

Then I smelled something else. It was...yes, it was definitely...*pickles*.

"That was me, everybody," my sister cried, laughing uncontrollably.

Everyone else laughed, too.

CHAPTER 28

The End

And that's how it happened. That's how everything changed. If life gives you lemons, make lemonade. The saying is true. I was sick of bad gas. And it wasn't easy, but I figured out a way, with a lot of help, to fix it once and for all.

That's the whole story. The only other surprise that I haven't told you about is the money. It turned out that Sweet Farts became the fastest-selling product in history. Before we knew it, my family had made over one hundred million dollars! I even donated a lifetime supply to the Papas family.

I decided to start my own company with all that money. I work with Mr. Gonzalez at the laboratory, and I get to try any experiment I want. I also get to hire whoever I want. Scott was the first person I hired. The second was Anthony Papas. I figured if it weren't for him, I would have never invented Sweet Farts in the first place. We are working on some really cool experiments right now. I'd tell you about them, but they're confidential. Let's just say, the next time a kid in your class vomits on the floor right in the middle of class, you may not have to hold your nose. I've always hated that smell, haven't you?

Lemons to lemonade, my friends. Lemons to lemonade...

About the Author

Raymond Bean is the Amazon best-selling author of the Sweet Farts series. Writing for kids who claim they don't like reading, his books have ranked #1 in children's humor, humorous series, and fantasy and adventure genres, and the Sweet Farts series is consistently in Amazon's top 100 books for children. His second book, *Sweet Farts #2: Rippin' It Old School*, was Amazon Publishing's very first children's release. Foreign editions of his books have been released in Germany and Korea, and editions for Italy, Brazil, and Turkey are forthcoming.